STAR WARS™
THE FORCE AWAKENS
NEW ADVENTURES

Written by David Fentiman

Written and Edited by David Fentiman
Project Art Editor Owen Bennett
Creative Technical Support Tom Morse
Senior Designer David McDonald
Slipcase Designer Stefan Georgiou
Pre-Production Producer Kavita Varma
Senior Producer Alex Bell
Managing Editor Sadie Smith
Managing Art Editor Ron Stobbart
Creative Manager Sarah Harland
Art Director Lisa Lanzarini
Publisher Julie Ferris
Publishing Director Simon Beecroft

For Cameron + Company
Designers Dagmar Trojanek, Amy Wheless and Jillian Lungaro
Creative Director Iain Morris

For Lucasfilm
Executive Editor Jonathan W. Rinzler
Image Archives Stacey Leong
Art Director Troy Alders
Story Group Leland Chee, Pablo Hidalgo and Rayne Roberts

This edition published in 2016
First published in Great Britain in 2015
by Dorling Kindersley Limited,
80 Strand, London, WC2R 0RL

Slipcase UI: 001-305124-Oct/16

Page design copyright © 2016 Dorling Kindersley Limited.
A Penguin Random House Company

A CIP catalogue record for this book
is available from the British Library

ISBN: 978-0-2412-0115-2

Printed in China.

www.dk.com
www.starwars.com

A WORLD OF IDEAS:
SEE ALL THERE IS TO KNOW

Contents

A NEW BATTLE

The galaxy is in danger!
The evil First Order wants to take over.
Only the Resistance can stop it.

THE RESISTANCE

The brave Resistance fights against the First Order.
General Leia is the leader of the Resistance. She has
many pilots and soldiers to help her. The Resistance
has a secret base on a planet named D'Qar.

THE FIRST ORDER

The First Order is all that remains of the Empire. The evil Empire once ruled the galaxy. It was destroyed many years ago by Leia and her brother, Luke. Now the First Order wants revenge!

Kylo Ren

Kylo Ren is the First Order's greatest warrior. He is very powerful, and very evil. Kylo uses a weapon known as a lightsaber. He also uses the Force. This is a strange energy that gives him special powers!

General Leia

General Leia is also a princess. Many years ago, she fought against the Empire with her brother, Luke. He was a noble warrior known as a Jedi. Luke disappeared a long time ago, and now Leia is trying to find him.

C-3PO and R2-D2

R2-D2 and C-3PO are old friends of Leia's. They are both droids. C-3PO serves Leia in the Resistance, but R2-D2 has been shut down for a long time. Ever since his master Luke Skywalker went away, R2 has not spoken to anyone.

Poe Dameron

Poe is General Leia's best pilot. His ship is called an X-wing. Poe flies his X-wing with great skill. Leia sends Poe on a secret mission to help find her brother, Luke. Poe is very brave and would do anything for Leia.

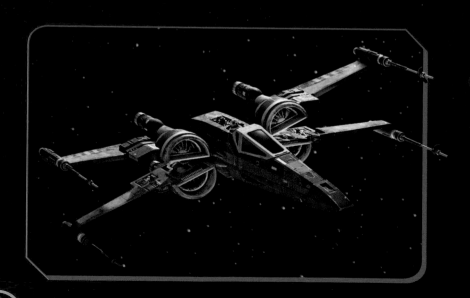

POE'S MISSION

MISSION GOAL 1

Fly to desert planet
named Jakku

MISSION GOAL 2

Meet the explorer
Lor San Tekka

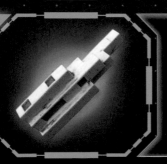

MISSION GOAL 3

Get secret artefact
from Lor and bring
it back to Leia

MISSION PLANET Jakku

POSSIBLE DANGERS

- First Order might attack at any time
- Jakku has savage wildlife and dangerous deserts

Finn

Finn was once a stormtrooper. Stormtroopers are the First Order's soldiers. His real name is FN-2187, but his friends call him Finn. Finn sees how evil the First Order is, and he decides to run away.

Rey

Rey comes from the planet Jakku. She works in a junkyard, and never expects to join the Resistance. Rey is an expert at fixing machines. She has built a speeder out of spare parts. Rey slowly realises that she can use the Force.

BB-8

BB-8 is a type of robot called
an astromech droid. He helps
Poe pilot his X-wing. BB-8 is
an unusual droid. His whole
body rolls when he moves,
but his head stays still!
BB-8 is very loyal to Poe.

THE FIRST ORDER

BE FEARLESS

FOLLOW ORDERS

TRUST YOUR LEADERS

Captain Phasma

Captain Phasma leads the First
Order's stormtroopers. She wears
special silver armour and is very
frightening. The only thing she
cares about is destroying the
First Order's enemies.

General Hux

General Hux is in charge of the
First Order's army and fleet of
starships. Hux has built a huge
weapon named the Starkiller.
He wants to use it to defeat
the Resistance.

THE STARKILLER

The Starkiller is a giant weapon. It takes up
a whole planet! It can smash an entire star
system with a single blast. The Starkiller
is guarded by thousands of stormtroopers.

- ▶ Able to destroy
  an entire star system
- ▶ Shields are very strong
- ▶ Has very powerful
  defences

- ▶ Cannot move
- ▶ Cannot be hidden
- ▶ If damaged, may
  destroy itself
- ▶ Takes time to charge up

The Resistance Base

The Resistance base is hidden
on a planet named D'Qar.
The base is where the Resistance
keeps its starships.

The Resistance base also has a command centre. It is buried deep underground. This is where General Leia and her officers plan their battles.

Admiral Statura

Admiral Statura is General Leia's second-in-command at the Resistance base. He helps Leia plan missions against the First Order. Admiral Statura is very clever. He knows a lot about weapons and vehicles.

Han Solo and Chewbacca

Han was once a smuggler, but he helped Leia defeat the Empire. He and his co-pilot Chewbacca have been together for a very long time. Their ship is called the *Millennium Falcon*. Han cares for Leia, and he agrees to join the Resistance.

Admiral Ackbar

Admiral Ackbar is one of Leia's officers. He is a Mon Calamari.

He fought beside Leia in the war against the Empire, 30 years ago. They have been through many dangerous battles together. Leia trusts Ackbar with her life.

PILOT PROFILE
Poe Dameron

RANK: **Commander**

HOMEWORLD: **Yavin 4**

SKILL: **Improvising**

PILOT PROFILE
Snap Wexley

RANK: **Captain**

HOMEWORLD: **Akiva**

SKILL: **Scouting missions**

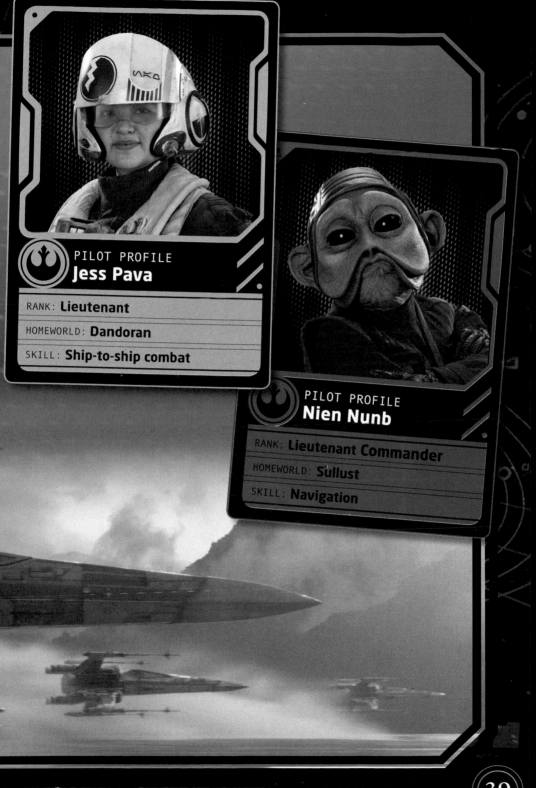

PILOT PROFILE
Jess Pava

RANK: **Lieutenant**

HOMEWORLD: **Dandoran**

SKILL: **Ship-to-ship combat**

PILOT PROFILE
Nien Nunb

RANK: **Lieutenant Commander**

HOMEWORLD: **Sullust**

SKILL: **Navigation**

X-WINGS

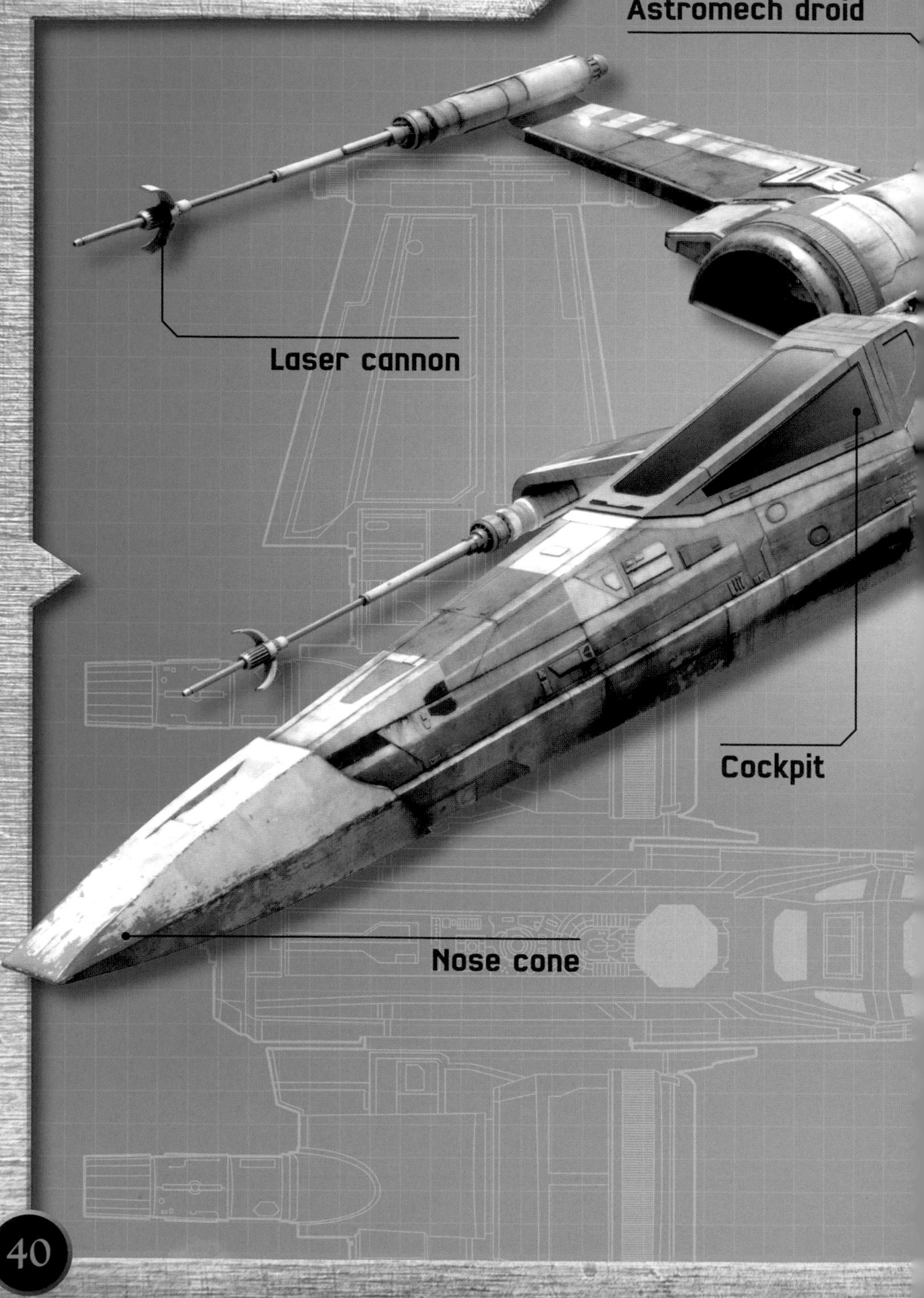

Astromech droid

Laser cannon

Cockpit

Nose cone

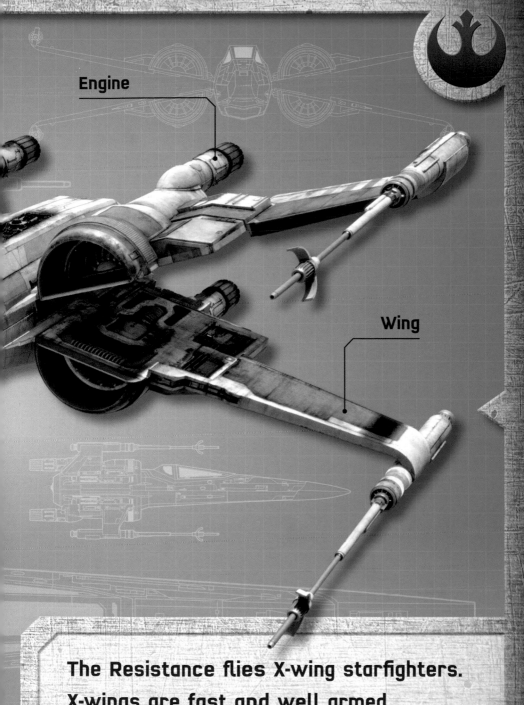

Engine

Wing

The Resistance flies X-wing starfighters.
X-wings are fast and well armed.
The X-wing pilots must try to
destroy the Starkiller!

Quiz

1. Who is the First Order's greatest warrior?

2. Who leads the Resistance?

3. What is the First Order's giant weapon called?

4. What type of droid is BB-8?

Quiz

5. What kind of starfighters does the Resistance use?

6. What is Finn's real name?

7. Where does Rey work?

8. Who is General Leia's best pilot?

Answers on page 47

Glossary

Droid A robot

The Empire An evil group that once ruled the galaxy

The First Order A powerful army created from the remains of the Empire

The Force A strange and powerful energy that has a light side and a dark side

General Someone who leads soldiers in battle

Jedi Someone who uses the light side of the Force to do good

The Resistance A group that defends the galaxy from the First Order

Smuggler Someone who transports illegal goods

Index

Answers to the quiz on pages 42 to 45:
1. Kylo Ren 2. General Leia 3. The Starkiller
4. An astromech droid 5. X-wings 6. FN-2187
7. A junkyard 8. Poe Dameron

A Note to Parents

DK READERS is a compelling programme for beginning readers, designed in conjunction with leading literacy experts, including Maureen Fernandes, B.Ed (Hons). Maureen has spent many years teaching literacy, both in the classroom and as a consultant in schools.

Beautiful illustrations and superb full-colour photographs combine with engaging, easy-to-read stories to offer a fresh approach to each subject in the series. Each DK READER is guaranteed to capture a child's interest while developing his or her reading skills, general knowledge, and love of reading.

The five levels of DK READERS are aimed at different reading abilities, enabling you to choose the books that are exactly right for your child:

Pre-level 1: Learning to read
Level 1: Beginning to read
Level 2: Beginning to read alone
Level 3: Reading alone
Level 4: Proficient readers

The "normal" age at which a child begins to read can be anywhere from three to eight years old. Adult participation through the lower levels is very helpful for providing encouragement, discussing storylines, and sounding out unfamiliar words.

No matter which level you select, you can be sure that you are helping your child learn to read, then read to learn!